The Big Monkey Mix-up

Avon Books are available at special quantity discounts for bulk
purchases for sales promotions, premiums, fund raising or educa-
tional use. Special books, or book excerpts, can also be created to
fit specific needs.

For details write or telephone the office of the Director of Special
Markets, Avon Books, Dept. FP, 1350 Avenue of the Americas,
New York, New York 10019, 1-800-238-0658.

The Big Monkey Mix-up

Pamela Jane

Illustrations by Cathy Bobak

AN AVON C CAMELOT BOOK

AVON BOOKS
A division of
The Hearst Corporation
1350 Avenue of the Americas
New York, New York 10019

Copyright © 1997 by Pamela Jane
Interior illustrations copyright © 1997 by Avon Books
Interior illustrations by Cathy Bobak
Published by arrangement with the author
Visit our website at http://AvonBooks.com
Library of Congress Catalog Card Number: 97-93051
ISBN: 0-380-78951-5
RL: 2.1

First Avon Camelot Printing: September 1997

CAMELOT TRADEMARK REG. U.S. PAT. OFF. AND IN OTHER COUNTRIES, MARCA REGISTRADA, HECHO EN U.S.A.

Printed in the U.S.A.

OPM   10 9 8 7 6 5 4 3 2 1

To John, Cathy, Lara, and Evan—
for old and new times' sake.

—P. J.

Contents

The Big Monkey Mix-up

1

The Flying Tooth

Benjamin was happy. His best friend, Mike Angelo, had moved back across the street.

Mike's family had moved to New York last summer when his father got a new job. But now Mr. Angelo had his old job back, and Benjamin had a best friend again.

That was the good part. The bad part was that Mike had a loose tooth. That wouldn't have been bad, except for one thing.

Benjamin hadn't lost a single tooth, even now that he was in second grade. All his baby teeth were hanging on for dear life!

Everyone else in Mike and Benjamin's class had missing teeth. Last week Amy lost her front tooth. The next morning she came to school, proudly waving the dollar the Tooth Fairy had left her. Then the class sang Amy the Tooth Fairy song:

The Tooth Fairy has come
Let us all sing and shout
She left Amy a gift
For the tooth that came out!

Benjamin felt left out. No one would ever sing him the Tooth Fairy song. He'd be a hundred years old and still have all his baby teeth.

Mrs. Humphrey, Benjamin's mother, wasn't worried.

"You're a late bloomer," she said. "Bilo is the same way." Bilo was Benjamin's baby sister.

Benjamin frowned. He did not like being compared to someone who spit up and wet her pants.

"Bilo is eight months old, and she hasn't grown a single tooth," said Mrs. Humphrey, with a smile. "But I'm not worried. Everything happens at the right time."

"But this *is* the right time," said Benjamin, "and nothing is happening. Not one tooth is even a tiny bit loose!"

At that moment Benjamin's big sister, Slug, walked in, swinging a hammer. She and her friends, Katie and Heather, were building a new clubhouse in the backyard.

Slug's real name was Victoria. But no one called her that.

Slug grinned at Benjamin. "I'll give you a loose tooth," she said. "All I have to do is slug you!"

"Very funny," said Benjamin. And he stomped upstairs to his room.

Benjamin was mad at Slug. He was also mad at the Tooth Fairy. A fairy should help people. This one was too busy leaving dollars for other kids.

The next day Mike had a surprise—another loose tooth! It was his fourth one.

Benjamin felt more left out than ever. All Mike talked about was his new loose tooth! He wiggled it in front of the class during Share Time. At recess he hung upside down on the jungle gym and rocked it back and forth. By lunch time it was hanging by a thread.

"Watch, everyone!" shouted Mike, standing up in the crowded cafeteria. "I'm going to pull my tooth out!"

Benjamin's noisy lunch table suddenly grew quiet. All eyes were on Mike.

Mike grabbed his tooth.

"Bet you won't do it!" said Jack Rock.

"Bet I will!" said Mike. But Benjamin thought Mike looked a little scared now that everyone was watching.

"Hurry up," shouted Amy, "do it!"

"I can't look!" said Benita, squeezing her eyes shut.

Mike closed his eyes and took a deep breath. Jack sneaked up behind him, grinning.

"Mike, watch out!" Benjamin yelled. But it was too late. Jack gave Mike a shove. Mike lurched forward and his tooth popped out—and went flying!

2

Benjamin Acts Fast

Mike opened his eyes.

"My tooth!" he cried. "I lost my tooth!"

Just then the bell rang. Lunch hour was over.

"Second graders, line up!" called Mrs. Meltzer, the lunch monitor.

Mike was running around wildly, searching for his tooth. Benjamin helped.

"Come along, you two!" Mrs. Meltzer called.

"But I lost my tooth!" said Mike. "I have to find it."

Mr. Oliver, the school custodian, began pushing tables and chairs against the wall for fourth-grade gym. Mike rushed over to him.

"Have you seen my tooth?" he asked.

Mr. Oliver smiled.

"No, let me see it," he said, bending over to look in Mike's mouth.

"No, I mean the tooth I lost!" said Mike. "It came out right here, in the cafeteria."

Mr. Oliver shook his head.

"Nope, I haven't found any teeth," he said. "But I'll let you know if I do."

Mike walked away sadly.

That was when it happened.

Benjamin was turning to go when he noticed something small and white on the floor. The missing tooth!

"Hey, Mike!" cried Benjamin.

But Mike was already halfway across the cafeteria and didn't hear him.

And then Benjamin did something he wished later he had never done at all.

Quickly, before anyone could see him, Benjamin picked up Mike's tooth and dropped it deep into his own pocket.

3

One Mean Jellybean

Of course, Benjamin planned to give Mike's tooth back. But first he wanted to see, just once, how it felt to have a tooth out.

The minute he got home, Benjamin locked himself in the bathroom and took the tooth out of his pocket. He was surprised at how small it was. All that fuss over a tiny little tooth!

Benjamin pretended to show off his new missing tooth in front of the mirror.

"Look!" he cried, "I lost a tooth!"

Benjamin grinned. Wouldn't his friends be surprised!

Suddenly a thought struck him. Why not bring the tooth to school and say it was his? After all, Mike had three missing teeth already, and Benjamin didn't have any.

That night when he was waiting to fall asleep, Benjamin remembered what his mother had said.

"Everything happens at the right time."

That might be true. But some things, thought Benjamin, smiling to himself, need a little help along the way.

*   *   *

First thing the next morning, Benjamin tiptoed to his closet and took out the bag of jellybeans he'd been hiding from Slug.

Benjamin peered into the bag. There were four green jellybeans left, three reds, and one black.

"*Yes!*" whispered Benjamin when he saw the black jellybean.

That jellybean was going to make his day—and a dollar, too.

As soon as Benjamin got to school, he

rushed to the boys' room. No one else was around. Standing in front of the mirror, Benjamin stuck the black jellybean to his back tooth. He smiled broadly. That was one mean jellybean! It looked as though he really had a tooth missing.

If you didn't look too close.

4

The Tooth Fairy's Surprise

Back in the classroom, Benjamin broke the news.

"Look everybody!" he shouted, holding out Mike's tooth. "My tooth just came out!"

Mike looked surprised.

"That looks like my tooth," he said, peering at the tiny tooth in Benjamin's hand. "The one I lost in the cafeteria."

Benjamin said nothing.

"Let's see where it came out," said
Amy.

Benjamin opened his mouth just a
little.

"There," he said, pointing to his blacked-
out tooth.

Amy leaned closer, squinting through
her glasses.

"Open wider. I can't see it," she said.

Benjamin opened his mouth a little wider. Amy leaned a little closer.

"I still can't see it," she said.

"It's way back there," said Benjamin. He was getting nervous. The jellybean was starting to melt!

"Oh, I see it!" said Amy. "It looks weird."

"Way to go, Benjamin!" said Benita, slapping Benjamin on the back.

Benjamin gulped, and swallowed the jellybean.

Benjamin didn't tell his family about his missing tooth. He might be able to fool the Tooth Fairy with someone else's tooth, but he'd never be able to fool his mother.

That night, Benjamin put the tooth under his pillow. Then he fell asleep, dreaming of the crisp new dollar the Tooth Fairy would leave him.

But when he woke up, Benjamin got a surprise. The only thing under his pillow was the tooth he had put there the night before.

Benjamin had not fooled the Tooth Fairy. She knew that the tooth under his pillow wasn't Benjamin's. And she wasn't about to give him a dollar for it, either!

Benjamin felt awful. Taking Mike's tooth had been wrong. Deep down, he had known that all along. But now the Tooth Fairy knew it, too. Benjamin hoped she wasn't mad.

He had a feeling it was very bad to have a good fairy mad at you.

5

A Bad-Luck Sign

Benjamin had to think of a way to give Mike's tooth back, and get on the Tooth Fairy's good side.

Benjamin slipped Mike's tooth in his back pocket and went downstairs. In the kitchen, his mother was making pancakes. They smelled good. But when Benjamin sat down to eat, he jumped up with a yell.

"OWWWW!"

"What's wrong with *you*?" asked Slug.

"Nothing," said Benjamin. Something was wrong, though. Mike's tooth had bit him right through his pants!

Benjamin put the tooth in his shirt pocket, but it fell through a hole and rolled under the table. When Benjamin bent over to pick it up, he bumped his head.

"OWWWW!" he yelled again.

His mother turned around from the stove. "Benjamin, are you all right?"

"Yes," said Benjamin, rubbing his head. But he wasn't. The stolen tooth was bad luck. The sooner he got rid of it, the better.

Benjamin walked to school late so he wouldn't meet Mike. He didn't want to answer any questions about the Tooth Fairy.

As it turned out, Benjamin didn't have to worry. At school everyone had forgotten about his missing tooth. Something more exciting had happened in the meantime.

During the night, someone had broken into the school and turned Benjamin's classroom upside down.

"Just look at this mess!" said Mrs. Rickert, Benjamin's teacher.

Chalk and erasers were scattered everywhere. The wastebasket was knocked over and Mrs. Rickert's pencil cup was smashed.

"Mrs. Rickert, look!" cried Benjamin. Someone had chewed his science book to pieces and dumped all his crayons on the floor!

"I left a banana in my desk," said Jack, "and now look what's left!" Jack held up a banana peel.

"Whoever broke in left me a note,"

said Benita. She held up a piece of paper covered with strange writing. Everyone crowded around to see.

"It's written in code!" said Mike.

"It looks like scribbling to me," said Amy.

"Maybe it's ghost writing," said Benita.

"Ghosts don't eat bananas," said Jack.

"We had a ghost once who ate cat food," said Nicholas.

Benjamin didn't say anything. He was worried. The break-in was another bad-luck sign.

He had to get rid of Mike's tooth, before something *really* bad happened.

6

IT

Soon the whole school was talking about IT. Benita thought IT was a ghost. Jack thought IT was a hungry vampire. Amy was sure IT was a pirate searching for hidden treasure.

In the cafeteria, Mr. Oliver found pots and pans turned upside down, dishes broken, and spoons thrown on the floor. IT had broken into the storeroom, too, and sucked the jelly out of all the jelly donuts.

"I told you IT is a vampire!" said Mike. "Only IT sucks jelly instead of blood!"

IT had spilled a jar of pepper all over the school. Now everyone was sneezing.

Benjamin and his friends discussed IT during lunch.

"IT—*aah-CHOO!*—could be anyone," said Mike.

Benita's eyes widened. "IT could even be one of us!"

For some reason everyone looked at Jack. It was just like Jack to play a trick like that.

"*Aah-aahh-CHOO!*" said Jack.

Suddenly Benita screamed. "Look!" she cried, pointing across the cafeteria. "There's a tail sticking out from under the stage curtain!"

Benjamin looked but he didn't see anything.

"You're imagining things," said Jack.

Suddenly the loudspeaker crackled, and a voice blared through the cafeteria.

"It is important for everyone to stay calm and not panic," announced Mrs.

Peabody, the principal. "The culprit—*AAH-CHOO!*—will be found and punished!"

Benjamin didn't know if IT was a ghost, a vampire, or an angry Tooth Fairy. But he knew one thing. The trouble had started right after he had taken Mike's tooth. Benjamin had to get rid of that tooth NOW before it caused any more trouble.

Benjamin glanced around the lunch table. Everyone was busy talking. Quickly, he took Mike's tooth out of his pocket and dropped it on the floor. He waited a minute and then picked it up again.

"Hey, Mike!" he said. "Look what I found. Your missing tooth!"

Mike peered at the tooth. "Nope," he said. "That's not mine."

"What do you mean, it's not yours?" said Benjamin. "I found it right here in the cafeteria, where you lost it."

"It's not mine, though," said Mike. "I found my tooth. Actually, my mom found it in the cuff of my pants. It must have dropped in there when Jack pushed me."

Mike pulled a dollar out of his pocket.

"See?" he said, grinning, "the Tooth Fairy left me a dollar. I forgot to tell you because of all the excitement about IT."

Benjamin stared at the dollar in Mike's hand. "But if it's not your tooth, whose is it?" he asked.

Everyone at Benjamin's table became interested in the mystery tooth.

"It's not mine!" said Benita.

Benjamin checked to make sure none of his own teeth were missing. Nope, they were all there.

Jack looked closely at the tooth in Benjamin's hand.

"Benjamin," he said. "That tooth looks weird."

A shiver prickled the back of Benjamin's neck. He had a feeling he knew what Jack was going to say.

"What do you mean, *weird*?" asked Benita.

Jack lowered his voice. "Well," he whispered, "it just doesn't look *human*."

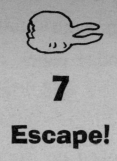

7

Escape!

Benjamin was sorry he had ever taken the tooth. All he wanted to do now was give it back. But how could he give it back when he didn't know who—or what—it belonged to?

Benjamin needed a plan. He decided to make a poster to advertise the lost tooth.

Benjamin sat down on the living room floor with crayons and a big poster board. **FOUND! ONE TOOTH!** he printed in bold letters.

Just then Benjamin's father, who was reading the Sunday paper, chuckled.

"Oh dear!" he said, "another animal on the loose."

Benjamin looked up from his poster.

"Did Max get out again?" he asked. Max the Moose had escaped from the local zoo several weeks before. When Benjamin captured him with leftover vegetables, the zoo had put on a parade in Benjamin's honor.

"It's not Max this time," said Benjamin's father. "It's a monkey."

"A monkey? What monkey?" said Slug, coming in from the backyard where she and her friends were working on their new clubhouse.

"Her name is Maggie," said Mr. Humphrey, reading from the paper. "She escaped from Monkey Island a few days ago."

"Wow!" said Slug, dropping her hammer. "Wait until I tell Katie and Heather. We'll make a trap and catch it!"

Benjamin jumped up to go tell Mike. But then he stopped.

"Dad," he said, "can I see that story about the monkey?"

"Sure, I'll just keep the sports section," his father said.

Benjamin sat down on the floor with the newspaper. Benjamin loved to read about animals. He read the story, sounding out the big words as he went along.

The newspaper said that Maggie was a young monkey. (In monkey years, she was probably about three.) She had belonged to an old organ grinder before she came to live at the zoo. Maggie and the organ grinder used to put on a show together. Benjamin liked that part.

Benjamin gazed thoughtfully at the newspaper headlines.

LOST! ONE MONKEY!

Then he looked at his poster.

FOUND! ONE TOOTH!

Suddenly something clicked in Benjamin's mind.

What if the mysterious tooth belonged to Maggie? That would mean that a monkey was loose in his school!

"Dad, do monkeys lose their baby teeth the way kids do?" asked Benjamin.

Mr. Humphrey looked up from the newspaper. "I never thought about it," he said. "But monkeys are mammals like we are, so I suppose they do."

Benjamin picked up a crayon and drew a big line through his poster. He was pretty sure he wouldn't be needing it now.

After all, monkeys can't read.

8

The Peanut Trap

Benjamin couldn't wait to tell Mike about Maggie and the mysterious tooth.

"It's a monkey tooth, I know it!" he said. He and Mike were sitting on Benjamin's front porch.

"It does look really small," said Mike. He stared hard at the tooth in Benjamin's hand. "You know what? I think it's a molar."

"A monkey molar!" said Benjamin.

Mike grinned. "Maggie is IT. She's the one who chewed up your science book and ate Jack's banana!"

"We've got to catch her," said Benjamin.

"Shhh!" whispered Mike. "Look who's coming."

Slug and Katie and Heather were walking down the street, carrying a large box. Wolf, Katie's dog, bounded behind.

"Where are you going with that box?" called Mike.

"None of your business," said Slug.

"None of your *monkey* business," said Katie. The three girls giggled.

"I bet you're going to make a trap to catch Maggie," said Benjamin.

"You caught the moose, Benjamin, but we're getting the monkey," said Heather.

Slug grinned. "The monkey will reach its paw in for the peanuts and then—ZAP! It'll be trapped!"

Mike and Benjamin watched the girls cross the street to Carter's Park, which was next to the zoo.

"They'll never catch Maggie with that dumb box," said Benjamin.

"But how are we going to catch her?" asked Mike. "We don't even know where she's hiding."

"Remember when Amy said she saw something sticking out from under the stage curtain?" asked Benjamin.

"A tail!" said Mike. "Maggie's hiding

behind the stage. She's too shy to come out.''

Benjamin frowned. ''She can't be that shy,'' he said. ''The newspaper said that Maggie used to put on a show with an organ grinder.''

''I saw an organ grinder with a monkey in a movie, once,'' said Mike. ''The monkey wore a funny little hat and a red coat. He danced and did tricks while the old man cranked a little organ.''

''Maybe if we did that, Maggie would come out and do tricks for us,'' said Benjamin. ''But where are we going to find one of those organs?''

''I have an old music box,'' said Mike.

"It plays music when you crank the handle."

"We'll sneak into the cafeteria with it, after school," said Benjamin.

Mike's eyes lit up. "I can't wait to see the principal's face when we catch IT!"

9

A Long Tail

Benjamin called Mike the next morning before he left for school.

"Do you have the music box?" he whispered.

"Got it!" Mike whispered back.

"What's all the whispering about?" demanded Slug, poking her head into the kitchen.

Slug was in a bad mood because Wolf, Katie's dog, had ripped open the monkey trap and gobbled up all the peanuts.

"I'll catch that monkey if it's the last thing I do," she had vowed.

Benjamin slipped out the back door, singing to himself. "Slug hasn't caught that monkey yet, but I'll catch Maggie soon, I bet!"

After school, Mike and Benjamin skipped Cub Scouts and hurried down to the cafeteria. It stood empty and quiet, the tables and chairs stacked neatly against the wall.

Mike took the music box out of his book bag while Benjamin stood guard at the door.

"All clear!" he called, peering down the hall.

Mike began to crank the handle of the music box. Circus music filled the air.

"I hope Maggie comes out soon, before someone hears us!" said Benjamin.

Mike kept cranking the music box, but there was no sign of Maggie.

Outside a cloud passed over the sun.

All at once the empty cafeteria seemed dark and spooky.

Mike looked around nervously.

"What if IT really is a ghost, or a vampire?" he whispered.

"Shhh!" hissed Benjamin. "Look!"

Peeking out from behind the stage cur-

tain were two bright eyes and a long tail. Maggie!

As Benjamin and Mike watched, the monkey came out and began dancing a jig on the stage.

"Stay here and keep cranking the music box," said Benjamin. "I'm going to call the zoo!"

10

The Good-Luck Tooth

By the time the zoo truck pulled up, the whole scout troop was in the cafeteria, along with Mrs. Rickert and Mrs. Peabody, the principal.

Mr. McCullers, the zoo curator, strode into the room, barking orders.

"Everybody calm down and stay quiet!"

The music stopped. Everybody stood still.

"You can come in now!" Mr. McCullers called to his crew.

In walked Dr. Hackberry, the animal doctor, and three helpers. One of the helpers had a cage. Two others carried nets with long handles.

When Maggie saw the nets, she leapt off the stage and began dashing around the cafeteria.

"*Cheeee! Cheeee!*" she screeched, as she swung from the gym-climbing ropes to the overhead rafters.

Mrs. Peabody gasped.

"Someone catch that monkey!" she cried.

"Quick—get the jelly donuts!" Mr. McCullers shouted to Dr. Hackberry.

"*Cheee! Cheee!*"

"Maggie, come down here this minute," called Mr. McCullers.

"*Cheee! Choo-choo-choo!*" trilled Maggie, swinging upside down from the basketball hoop.

"Just a little closer, Maggie!" coaxed Dr. Hackberry, holding out a jelly donut.

With a flying leap, Maggie swooped down, grabbed the donut from Dr. Hackberry, and swung back up to the rafters, screaming. The Cub Scout troop jumped up and down, yelling.

"Get the net!"

"Get a ladder!"

"*Wheet! Choo-choo-choo!*" sang Maggie. She was laughing at them!

Benjamin got an idea.

"Maybe if we play the music box, Maggie will come down and dance," he said.

Mike began cranking the music box. Maggie hopped up and down on the rafters, chattering. Suddenly she leapt down to the floor. The scout troop cheered. Maggie danced around. Then she jumped on Benjamin's shoulder and pretended to scratch his head. Everyone laughed.

"She's doing her act!" said Mike.

Mr. McCullers picked Maggie up gently and put her in her cage.

"Whew!" he said, wiping his forehead. "You two boys did it. You got our monkey!"

"Yay!" cheered the Cub Scouts.

Mrs. Peabody had to go sit down. Having a monkey loose in her school had shaken her up.

"What gave you the idea of playing music?" asked Mrs. Rickert.

"It said in the newspaper that Maggie used to put on a show with an organ grinder," Benjamin explained. "We didn't have an organ so we used a music box. When Maggie heard the music, she came out from behind the stage and started to dance."

Dr. Hackberry whistled softly. "So

that's why Maggie ran away!'' he said. ''She missed the old organ grinder and his music.''

''From now on, we're going to play music on Monkey Island,'' said Mr. McCullers. ''Maggie can dance all she wants. The visitors will love it.''

''*Cheee! Cheee*!'' chattered Maggie, clapping her paws together.

Benjamin went over to Maggie's cage.

''Good-bye, Maggie,'' he said. ''It was great having you visit our school.''

Maggie stuck her paw out of the cage and shook Benjamin's hand.

''*Tuk-Tuk*!'' she said softly. Benjamin was sure that meant ''Thank you.''

Before he left, Benjamin took Maggie's

tooth out of his pocket and handed it to
Mr. McCullers.

"I found this on the cafeteria floor,"
he said. "I think it belongs to Maggie."

"By George, that *is* a monkey tooth!"
said Dr. Hackberry.

Mr. McCullers handed the tooth back
to Benjamin.

"You keep it," he said, "for good luck."

Benjamin smiled and put the good-luck tooth back in his pocket.

11

A Big Bite

That night Benjamin's family took Benjamin and Mike out to dinner to celebrate Maggie's return.

"You boys order anything you want," said Mrs. Humphrey.

"What about me?" said Slug. "I would have caught Maggie if she hadn't been hiding in Benjamin's school. That trap we built was really good."

Benjamin and Mike had cheeseburg-

ers and french fries. For dessert Benjamin ordered brownie-fudge ice cream. He was biting into a cold, chewy brownie when he got a funny feeling in his mouth.

"Hey!" said Benjamin, "I have a loose tooth!"

"Congratulations!" said his mother.

"It's about time," said Slug.

"I'm not a late bloomer anymore!" cried Benjamin. "I'm right on time!"

Everyone laughed, even Baby Bilo. When Bilo laughed, Benjamin noticed something.

"Mom, Bilo has a new tooth. And it's right on the bottom, exactly where my old tooth is coming out!"

The story of Maggie's capture was big news in Benjamin's town. A few days later, a photographer came to take Mike and Benjamin's picture for the newspaper. Benjamin made sure his loose tooth was out in time for the picture (it took a lot of wiggling, but it was worth it). And he made *double-sure* he was smiling when

the flash went off. Benjamin's missing tooth was big news, too!

That night when he climbed into bed, Benjamin thought about what his mother had said.

"Everything happens at the right time."

His mother was right. Everything did happen at the right time—Benjamin's old tooth coming out, Bilo's new tooth coming in.

Before he turned out the light, Benjamin put his tooth under his pillow.

This time, he felt sure, the Tooth Fairy would come.

Hey, Everybody!

LET'S HAVE A PARTY

Have Your Own Party! Fun Tips in Every Book

#1 SCHOOL'S OUT!
78925-6/$3.99 US/$4.99 Can

#2 SPLASH!
78922-1/$3.99 US/$4.99 Can

#3 SLEEPOVER
78924-8/$3.99 US/$4.99 Can

#4 SURPRISE!
78921-3/$3.99 US/$4.99 Can

And coming soon
#5 BOO WHO?
79256-7/$3.99 US/$4.99 Can

#6 THANKSGIVING FIESTA
79257-5/$3.99 US/$4.99 Can

#7 SECRET SANTA
79258-3/$3.99 US/$4.99 Can

Read All the Stories by
Beverly Cleary